Written by
Davis G. See

HEART FOLD
press

ISBN - 9798233047848 (Print)

Written by Davis G. See
Published by Heartfelt Press
Text & Cover Design by Carlos Vargas

For those who are still finding the courage to step into the light. May you feel seen, may you feel loved, and may the world embrace you as beautifully as you are. Your journey is valid, and your time to shine is coming.

FRIDAY

Arcturus lies in pieces on the bed, his flat eyes gazing at the stucco ceiling from his detached head. I try to picture wearing him, covering my own face with his stark white fur and stepping out of this room. I want him to be seen, to be loved, but all I can imagine of are the harsh glares of the hotel staff or people on the street, gawking at the freak in a fursuit.

Apologizing silently, I leave him there.

I'm not the only one here out of costume, but ordinary humans like me mingle in about equal measure with folks wearing cat ears, fluffy tails, and full, furry suits. A bipedal wolf at the head of the line chats casually with convention staff as his plain-clothed companion pays for day passes. I'm glad I'm not the only one without ornamentation, but at the same time, I'm kicking myself. I could have been standing shoulder to shoulder with a serval and an ocelot as Arcturus. Then again, maybe my shoddy fursuit would pale in comparison to the suits here...

"You can go ahead, I think." A tall, wide, black-haired man addresses me. He gestures at the gap between me and the registration desk.

"Oh! Sorry." I rush ahead and fumble to unlock my phone and find proof of purchase buried in my email inbox. The guy at the desk hands me a badge and a marker. I write 'Alex' in the name box and flee into the convention centre.

I thought the suits outside were impressive, but the sheer mass of masterful costumes in the lobby is overwhelming. I stand gawking at the dragon with glowing green scales, deer with majestic antlers, and bat with full wingspan, scattered in amongst more dogs than I could shake a stick at, until someone bumps into me from behind. A space this crowded would be hard enough to walk in without the added obstructions of tails and snouts. I squeeze past a flock of colourful birds to take a bench against the wall.

To reorient myself, I open up the convention schedule on my phone. The panels I'm excited about don't start until later, so maybe I should find something relaxing until the morning crowds disperse... Looks like a quiet drawing hour just started in one of the meeting rooms. I gather up my courage and re-enter the ocean of furries, letting the current carry me to my destination.

By the time I emerge with a few more sketches of Arcturus added to my sketchbook, the lobby is a lot calmer. There are still some folks socializing here and there, but most people have scattered to actual convention activities.

The walk to my next panel is much less frenzied, and I can even admire an excellently crafted beagle suit without worrying about crashing into someone. The panel room is set up with chairs around a number of round tables. I take a seat at an empty table near the front. Doing nothing makes me anxious, so I pull out my phone and scroll social media, retaining none of it.

I feel someone sit beside me. I slide my eyes off my screen to see a man a full head taller than me. His scruffy black hair curls at the edges. I feel like I've seen him somewhere before... or maybe it's just that he's hot.

"Do you mind if I sit here?" he asks. "I like to be able to face the front."

“Um, yeah, I mean no, I don’t mind. No problem,” I manage to say.

“Great. Hey, didn’t I see you at the registration line this morning?”

Oh, so that’s how I know him.

“Yeah, sorry. I was fully zoned out. I’ve never been to one of these before, so it’s, um, a lot. I mean, I’ve been to conventions before, but not a... not a furry convention.” I hitch instinctively before the word furry, as if I’m not surrounded by furries right now and instead still occupy a world where it feels like a dirty word. I silently vow to work on that.

“Ah, a first-timer. Well, nice to meet you, Alex,” he says, peering for a second at my con badge. He twists in his chair and offers a hand. I shake it, my scrawny fingers engulfed by his full ones. “I’m Jamie. Are you here by yourself?”

“Yeah. A friend was supposed to attend with me, but she’s all the way in Montreal and I guess something came up with her family. I thought about backing out, but I had already bought the weekend pass, so... A-and anyway, I wanted to come,” I add, not wanting to sound like I’m attending under duress.

Jamie’s face doesn’t suggest he got that impression, but it doesn’t suggest much else, either. He just smiles. I cough. "What about you? You're alone, too?"

"I am, but I've been coming for a long time so I know basically everyone."

"Oh. That's great." But it makes me wonder why he sat with me.

A woman enters with a heavy-looking tote bag. She sets it down by the podium at the front, then looks around the room before spotting Jamie and grinning. "Jasper! What are you doing here? I don't think I'll be talking about anything you don't already know."

Jasper?

"It never hurts to brush up on the basics. But actually, Sabrina, there's something I wanted to ask you. I was getting my suit ready for this weekend and I noticed a tear..." He gets up and speaks quietly with her as she unpacks fabric and scissors and thread. Then he returns to his seat, and she takes the podium.

"Hello everyone, and welcome to Love and Fur: Fursuit Care and Repair 101! If you're here, you're probably a new fursuit owner," she says, looking pointedly at Jamie, "wondering things like, What do I do if I damage my suit? or, How the hell do I clean this thing? We'll be going over some key tips and techniques for helping your suit last until you're a wizened old greymuzzle, including some hands-on practice. For safety reasons, please use your human hands for those parts. Opposable thumbs are mandatory!"

She describes some common issues fursuit owners run into and how to address them, and I quickly pick up on multiple things I did wrong when making mine, but that's exactly what I'm here for. Then she hands out some fabric scraps and sewing supplies and lets us try out what we've been taught as she wanders the room, keeping an eye out for anyone who needs help. Jamie takes up the task confidently; I can tell this is nothing new for him.

Chatter fills the room as the other tables converse amongst themselves. I suppose it would be fine for me to talk a bit, too...

I clear my throat. Jamie glances at me without halting his needlework. "So, um, she called you Jasper before?" I ask.

"Jasper's my fursona. See?" He puts the needle down to lift a badge from his chest, separate from the convention badge.

This one is a laminated illustration of a dark brown bear with a fierce but playful expression, his sharp teeth gleaming. The name 'Jasper' is written across the bottom in angular letters. I take the badge in my hand and pull it closer for a better look.

“Whoa, I love him! I’ve seen a lot of bear fursonas online with exaggerated muscles, and those are great, don’t get me wrong, but I love how Jasper actually looks like he’s been preparing for winter.”

“Thanks. It was important to me that he have a body like mine,” says Jamie, quietly.

Then I notice the badge itself, the thick, sturdy feel of it between my fingers. “Man, I should get one of these. Oh, not a fursona, I have a fursona, obviously, but this badge is a great way to show it off.”

I look up from it and realize that, in examining the badge, I’ve leaned closer and closer to Jamie. Our faces are mere inches apart. His eyes are almost black, like Jasper the bear’s.

I drop the badge and sit back in my chair. “Sorry, I got a little too excited...” I return to my fabric, keeping my gaze on the tip of the needle.

There is silence at our table. The casual laughter of the folks around us feels like mockery.

Then Jamie’s voice comes in, deep and soothing. “Can I see your fursona?”

I look at him. He’s smiling gently. I didn’t ruin this.

"Yes, of course!"

I rush to get my sketchbook out of my backpack and flip to the middle pages, searching for the drawing I did last week. When I find it, I slide the book in front of Jamie, pushing his needlework to the side

"This is Arcturus, or Archie for short. He's an Arctic fox. They live really far north, like up by the North Pole, but they come down to northern Alberta, too. I have family up north so I've actually seen one in the wild, though it was sure hard to spot! The white fur helps them blend right in to the snow, but it's just so striking, too, isn't it? Oh, and I love how they have these rounded ears, and they're generally more compact than other foxes, which keeps them nice and warm. I've always loved the snow, so when I was coming up with Archie, it seemed like a perfect fit, and, um..." I realize I'm ranting again. I fall quiet. Jamie doesn't seem bothered, though. He's looking at my art so carefully, gently running his finger over my lines.

"You drew this yourself?" he asks.

"Yeah. I've always like drawing."

"That's great. My badge art was a commission, and I'm very happy with it, but it would be cool to be able to draw my fursona myself at this quality."

"Oh, thanks. I'm sure you could if you tried, though. It just takes practice..."

"Do you take commissions or anything?"

"No, no, I don't think I'm that good. And anyway, I wouldn't want to make it my job. Might make it less fun."

He finally turns his gaze from Archie to me. I'm sure my face is bright red. "That's understandable," he says, "but I think if you wanted to, you would do well. A lot of people would love their fursonas to look as good as this."

"Oh, I don't know..."

I swallow and try to recentre. Work talk. That's a bit less scary. "I'm in graphic design," I say. "Logos, promo art, that kind of thing. I like it. It's creative without crossing that line of turning my passion into work, you know?"

"You ever do website design?"

"Yeah. Well, some page elements and things, you know. My coworkers cover layout and stuff."

"Nice. I'm on the technical side of that, back-end coding for web development."

"I wonder if we've ever worked on the same website, without ever even talking to each other..." The idea of that kind of secret, fated connection with Jamie makes me giddy. I try to suppress the smile that I feel creeping up my cheeks.

Sabrina returns to her place behind the podium and guides us onto our next task, while my fabric lies forgotten and incomplete on the table.

As I rise to leave at the end of the panel, Jamie stops me with a gentle hand on my bare forearm.

"What's your schedule looking like after this?" he asks.

"Oh, um." It takes me a second to form coherent thoughts. "I was thinking I might go watch fursuit improv next, and then I wanna attend the fursona sharing circle."

"Darn, I've got a screening of old anthro cartoons, but I'll see you at the sharing circle for sure."

I want to tell him that I'm not committed to the improv show, that I'd happily watch old cartoons if it's with him, but that's definitely too much. Instead I say,

"Okay, see you there."

The improv show (a great showcase of physical comedy, with one ferret fursuiter in particular standing out as exceptionally hilarious) lets out early, and I speedwalk to the small room for the fursona sharing circle.

I'm the second one there, taking one of the dozen or so chairs arranged, fittingly, in a circle. No Jamie yet. I casually place my backpack on the chair to my left and wait.

A few more furries file in and take their seats across the circle from me. I try to look casual, tapping my foot lightly.

Two hyenas enter and sit, separated from me only by the chair with my bag. I wring my hands.

Another couple, these ones unsuited but for striped tails wagging behind them, take another two seats to my right. I gulp.

A group of three or four peek their heads in, say something about it being full, and move on. I exhale.

A lone wolf enters and eyes the chair with my backpack, but ultimately takes the only other remaining chair. I avoid his gaze, and try to send my thoughts to Jamie. If he doesn't show up soon, I'll have to give his spot to someone else...

A fursuiter enters and my heart drops. They're a golden retriever with kind eyes. I am about to make space for them when they go to the front of the room and begin writing on the whiteboard.

They're the host! They stay by the front instead of joining the circle. There's still a chance!

I hear a deep, familiar voice. "Hey Lake, got room for one more?"

It's Jamie! He really does know everyone. Lake the retriever scrutinizes the room. "I think we have one more spot..."

I raise my hand. "Jamie! Over here!"

He sees me and grins. I feel as light as air. I put my backpack at my feet so he can sit beside me. The circle's pretty tight, and he's a bigger guy, so his arm touches mine. I feel my skin forming goosebumps.

Lake closes the door. "Thank you all for joining me today." Their voice is silky smooth, the barrier of their fursuit softening their words further. "I've been in the fandom for a long time, and there is nothing I love more than hearing about other furries' fursonas. The creation process is often profoundly personal, our fursonas coming from deep in our psyches, representing our truest selves, or perhaps the versions of us we wish we were. Or, maybe you just had fun coming up with a cute animal character, and that's great, too. I like to keep this event small, so we all have time to explore the smallest details of our fursonas, and so that everyone may feel safe sharing feelings close to their hearts. Mr. Wolf, if you're comfortable, perhaps we can start with you."

The wolf, who goes by Fenrir, stands so we can all see his fursuit. He explains how he decided on the design, and how being Fenrir gave him confidence he never had before, confidence that has carried over into his daily life.

His suit is really cool, his dark fur tipped with fiery red, and I want to ask about the Norse mythology connection but can't get the words out before he sits down and the circle moves on.

Next are the tailed couple, two first-time con-goers like me, young lesbians who started as friends but fell in love after they imagined their raccoon fursonas as an item. It's a sweet story, and I like how their relationship and their fursonas' relationship are different but still loving.

Then it falls to me. Suddenly I'm so nervous my hands shake as I fetch my sketchbook from my bag. I turn it to the page I showed Jamie and pass it to my right, and then I begin, telling everyone what I told Jamie, about Arcturus and why I made him an Arctic fox. Talking gets easier the more I share.

"Archie isn't really me," I say as my drawing of him travels around the circle. "I started making him because it seemed like it would be fun, and I loved the process of thinking through all the details of his life and design and personality so much that I wanted to share him with the world. He's my proudest creation. It's kind of like... he's my child." I've never admitted that before. I glance at Jamie, who smiles kindly. He passes my sketchbook back to me. When I take it, we graze fingertips.

Then it's Jamie's turn. He removes his badge, the one with art of Jasper, and sends it around the circle.

"That there is Jasper, a North American grizzly bear. If you've ever been camping and met a grizzly bear, you know that they are absolutely unbothered, they just go about their business and barely care whether you're there or not. When I was eighteen and coming up with my fursona, that's how I wanted to be. Everything about my life and self felt like a nuisance, to myself and others. Sometimes when people make their fursonas, they craft an ideal body, but what I most wanted was to be okay with my body as it was. After all, I find that heft charming on bears, so why couldn't I feel that way about mine? What surprised me, though, was that through every iteration, I could not imagine my fursona—this encapsulation of who I most wished I was—as anything but male.

If I hadn't become a furry, I never would have realized I was trans. Now I'm living as a man, I feel good about my body, and I feel good about myself. I'm confident, I have a wide variety of skills, and contributing to this community helps me not to feel like such a nuisance. And I owe it all to Jasper."

The circle falls silent. I'm in awe of Jamie's story. His badge reaches me, and Jasper's eyes pierce me, somehow both beady and deep. I pass him back to Jamie. "I'm glad you found him," I say.

"Yeah," says Jamie. "I am, too."

The circle continues until everyone's shared their story, and then they all begin to shuffle out, but I'm rooted to my seat. Jamie hasn't moved yet, either.

"Hey, I'm dipping out early today," he says. "I gotta go home and feed my cat since my sitter couldn't make it today. And I have to fix up my suit a bit for tomorrow."

"Oh yeah, you mentioned that at the care and repair panel."

"Speaking of tomorrow, will I get to meet Arcturus properly?"

I nearly gasp. "Yes! Actually, I was going to wear him today, but..." I don't know how to explain that

I chickened out. I don't want Jamie to think of me that way.

"Good," he says, "I'm excited to see him." Jamie pats my knee, sending a shiver up my leg, then stands. "All right, see you."

I'm happy I met you. I'm psyched to spend more time with you. I'm so impressed by you. I never want this weekend to end.

I can't say any of those things but can't come up with anything normal. As Jamie turns and steps away, I manage a weak, "Yeah, see you." He turns the corner, and I am left alone. I let my head fall into my hands.

My stomach aches. I completely forgot about lunch. I decide to leave the con early, too, grabbing a couple slices of pizza at the cafeteria on the way out and taking them up to my hotel room.

After eating, I lie on the bed next to Arcturus.

"Tomorrow," I tell him. "Tomorrow's your big debut."

I wonder what Jamie will think of him. I wonder what Jamie thinks of me. He has a lot of friends in the community, so I'm probably nothing special to him. Of course he'd be friendly to the newbie. Maybe he saw how frazzled I was in the registration line and took pity on me.

But the way he touched my arm, touched my knee... I flex my fingers in front of me. I want to touch him, too.

Groaning, I bury my face in Archie's torso. I'm being ridiculous. He's essentially a stranger, and I'll be going home when the convention's over. I was only drawn to him because I'm alone. That's all it was. Probably.

Exhausted, I fall asleep like that, on top of the hotel bed, still in my clothes, using my empty fursuit as a pillow.

SATURDAY

In the shower the next morning, I vow not to cling to Jamie like a parasite, to be friendly but not simpering.

I get dressed, and then stand for a moment with Arcturus's head in my hands. I'm determined not to be a coward again, to do what I came here for. It takes a minute, but I find some mental fortitude and slip Archie's face over my own.

There are sounds in the hallway, a small group exiting their room. Fellow furries? I rush to the door and peer out the peephole. Though it's difficult to see through such a small opening and Archie's eyes, I think I make out non-human, bipedal creatures by the elevator. I quickly exit and stroll over as the elevator doors open. The fursuiters greet me and let me get on with them.

Some of my tension leaves me as the elevator descends. This should be okay. If I'm not the only one who looks like this, then the short walk to the convention centre should be just fine.

I stick with the group, ignoring the pointed fingers of passersby, until I flash my badge at the convention entrance and split off in the lobby. There's a noticeable difference between the beating summer heat outside and the air-conditioned convention hall. I was worried, but Arcturus should be fairly comfortable as long as I stay indoors.

It's not as packed in here today without the frenzy of first-day registration. Looking around, I don't notice Jamie, or any bears. Well, that's fine. If I see him, I see him, I tell myself.

I step to the side and pull my arm out of Archie's and into his torso so I can retrieve my phone from my jean pocket and hold it inside Archie's head, way too close to my face. According to the schedule, the fursuit parade isn't until later this afternoon. The thought of marching around with Arcturus on display is thrilling and nerve-wracking. If I want to show him off, that's the way to do it.

I mentally commit. No matter how scary it is, I'm doing it. Until then, I decide to go with the flow, starting with a stroll through the vendor hall.

Now this room is packed, despite being massive. I'm used to busy vendor halls with people obstructing traffic by milling around to look at the merchandise; that's the same as any convention. What I'm not used to is wearing Arcturus. He's not all that bulky compared to a lot of other fursuits, but he still adds to my width just enough that I keep bumping shoulders with other furries. I adjust pretty quickly, though. Soon I'm navigating the hall without issue, checking out fursuit supplies, clothing, comics, accessories, and more furry stuff than I knew existed.

What I'm really curious about, though, is the artists' alley, which I find in a separate hall just off the vendor hall. I've been to cons where the artists' alley really is just an alley, a single strip of tables for a select few illustrators, but here there's almost as much space as the main vendor hall. I slow way down to peruse every table. The diversity is striking, from modern cartoony characters to grand fantasy scenes that position mice or rabbits as sword-wielding heroes.

I pause at a sci-fi artist's table to flip through a whole binder full of lush illustrations. Behind me, I overhear bits and pieces of a conversation, voices muffled by fursuits.

"...is spectacular, don't you think, Jasper?"

Jasper?! I spin around. At the table across from me stands a hulking brown bear, conversing with some sort of antlered rabbit. That's gotta be him. Before I can think to stop myself, I've crossed the gap between us.

"Jasper!"

He turns at the sound of my voice. Jamie's face can't be seen under the head of Jasper, but that barely matters. His posture changes, and his hands—paws, rather, ending in shiny black claws—go up in surprise.

"Could it be... Arcturus?!"

I'm glad you recognize me."

"The white coat is very distinctive. It's just like you drew it."

I rub the back of my head with my paw. "Thanks. I made the suit myself, too. I know it could use improvement in a lot of ways, but if there's one thing I can vouch for, it's accuracy to Archie's design."

"You say that, but it's quite good. I never would have guessed it was your first attempt at a suit."

He makes a big show of moving his head this way and that to get a good look at me. I feel myself going red, and I'm glad he can't see my face.

"Ahem." The rabbit stands with his arms crossed. Like with me and Jamie, his face can't be seen, but his body language makes his annoyance clear.

"Arcturus," says Jamie, "this is my friend, Herrick. Herrick, this is Arcturus, who I met yesterday."

"Call me Archie," I say.

"Mm. And you're, what, an Arctic fox?" asks Herrick. I don't love his tone.

"Um, yes."

"But given the time of year, your coat shouldn't be this... shimmering white, should it?"

It's not a question he wants me to answer. He knows that I know that Arctic foxes get darker in the warmer months. My paws clench like fists.

"Hey Herrick," says Jamie kindly, "maybe you're not one to be critiquing on the basis of biological accuracy when there is, in fact, no such thing as a jackalope."

"Oh, a jackalope!" I say. "Yeah, I see it now. That's cool!"

"Hmph." Herrick touches the base of his antler.

"I think I'll show Archie around, since it's his first year," says Jamie, planting a thick paw on my shoulder. "If you're interested?"

"YES!"

That was too enthusiastic.

I bring my voice down. "Yes, I'd like that."

"Suit yourself," says Herrick, turning his attention to a stand covered in keychains.

Jamie lowers his head close to Archie's rounded ear. "Let's find somewhere quieter to talk. Okay?"

I nod, then gulp. Jamie leads the way out of the artists' alley, his bulk clearing traffic effortlessly.

We sit across from each other at a table in an empty meeting room. Apparently a panel was cancelled when the person running it came down with something.

"I'm glad I got to see you again," says Jamie.

"Oh. Um." Did he really just say that? My mouth opens and closes like a fish, but no sound comes out.

"I really did want to see you as Arcturus."

Oh, of course that's what he meant. "I know it's not perfect, but—"

"You've got to stop saying that. No one's expecting perfection, but I'm sure impressed. Especially since you made it yourself. This was a commission," he says, gesturing towards himself.

"Wait, really? It seemed like you knew a lot about sewing and stuff."

"I've picked up some skills to keep this in tip-top shape, but I could never make a whole fursuit from scratch. You're leagues ahead of me in that regard."

I grip the edge of the table with my paws. "I just... wanted to bring Arcturus to life, with my own hands. That's all."

"Well, it's damn impressive."

I don't know how to deal with all this praise he's heaping on me. Once again I'm glad to have my face hidden. "So Herrick is a friend of yours?" I ask, directing the conversation elsewhere.

"I wouldn't say we're close."

"Ah."

"I've been coming to this long enough that I know a lot of the regulars. But, to be honest, I can count on one paw the amount I talk to outside of convention weekend."

"Oh. Um, why is that?"

He shrugs, his furry brown shoulders heaving. "I don't know. Somehow all the relationships I form during convention weekend just... wash away.

Maybe a big bear like me is too intimidating to truly get close to?"

"No, no way," I say. "I mean, I want to get close to... you..." I trail off. That was definitely too much.

Forget Jasper the scary bear, I'm the one who's gonna scare him off. I study the surface of the table and wait for him to leave.

"...hey," he says. "It's almost time for the fursuit parade." Here it is, he's going to tell me he has to run off to prepare and leave me here to— "You're participating, yeah?"

I look up. "Huh?"

"I mean, you have to, right?"

"Did you... want me to?"

"I thought you wanted to share Arcturus with the world."

"I... I did. I do."

"Well then." He rises from the table, his furry form towering over me, and offers me a paw. Though his face isn't visible, I get the feeling that he's smiling.

"Shall we?"

The ballroom fills up with nearly every fursuiter at the convention, animals of all stripes converging for a single purpose. An excited energy abounds.

Furries in dog suits run around in circles, avians flap their wings, and wolves howl at the ceiling.

My nerves melt away. Everyone's just happy to be here. No one's going to notice that my suit was made by an amateur. All that matters is that I, and Arcturus, are here, a part of something.

When the time comes, we begin. We march in a long procession out of the ballroom and across the convention centre. We pass through the lobby and into the vendor hall, where we weave between booths. Shoppers stand aside to make way, and everyone we see, from the few fursuiters who didn't join to the vendors to the attendees in human clothes, cheer. They cheer and applaud and wolf whistle, all for us.

And all the while, Jamie walks beside me, waving at spectators with his big right paw. I find myself wanting to take his other paw in mine, to hold hands as we stride forward. But I can't do it. He doesn't get close to people, he said as much. I should just take this for what it is, a flash-in-the-pan friendship for one weekend only. I turn my attention back to the onlookers.

Then I feel something underneath me and before I understand what's happening I'm six feet taller. In a panic, I reach for something to hold onto and find two fuzzy bear ears. Jamie has lifted me onto his shoulders. I'm high above the rest of the paraders, fully visible, not lost in the crowd. Jamie knew I wanted to show off Arcturus, and he's making sure we're seen. The crowd goes wild, and I can't believe it's for Archie. For me.

Afterwards, Jamie and I grab some burgers and sit together in the cafeteria. We remove the heads of our fursuits and set them aside. I feel weirdly naked showing my face now, and maybe Jamie does, too.

Neither of us speaks as we eat, but I keep looking up from my food to catch him staring at me. Then he just smiles and looks away. I don't know what he's thinking when he looks at me, but I know what comes to mind when I see him: this man is gorgeous, in or out of his fursuit. If only I could say it.

The burgers disappear and our animal heads return, and our words with them. "What's next?" I ask.

"Well... We'd be just in time for tonight's dance," says Jamie.

I've never been one for dancing, always too self-conscious about the way my body moves... but Arcturus would love it. I decide to embody him, to be brave. "Sure, let's do it!"

"Okay."

He doesn't sound thrilled. His form is square and stiff.

"Do you like to dance?" I ask.

"Not normally... but Jasper is unbothered by the idea of people watching him, so I'll be okay."

Ah, so he's in the same boat as me. I grin. "Let's have fun, for Jasper and Archie's sake."

At that, he seems to relax, his shoulders dropping. "Yeah. Let's go."

We enter a wide, open hall, dimly illuminated, soft lights of all colours sweeping across the floor. A deer DJ stands behind a laptop on stage, while furries of all sorts lean against walls, chat by the punch bowl, or dance their hearts out, fuzzy limbs flying every which way to music that buzzes with bass. It's a lot like what I remember high school dances to be like, although with a very different dress code.

Jamie and I step together, one foot after the other, onto the dance floor.

But we don't know what to do with ourselves once we get there. We face each other, swaying gracelessly. I make up my mind to do what Arcturus would do and start dancing in earnest, swinging my arms and hopping back and forth.

It's awkward at first, but the movement carries itself, and soon that hesitation evaporates. Seeing me get into it, Jamie laughs and follows my lead. He does jazz hands with his paws, his claws wiggling, and I can't help but giggle.

I stand on tip toes, lean close to him, and shout to make myself heard over the music and through our suits. "I'm having a really good time with you," I say, or maybe it's Archie who says it. It doesn't feel like something I'd be able to say without him.

Jamie bends close to me in turn. "Me, too," he says, and I feel my insides light up. That energy keeps us dancing, with only brief breaks to hydrate and catch our breaths before getting back out there.

Eventually, the volume lowers and the lights dim further. Is it over? If so, time really slipped away from me. What's more, I don't feel ready to quit yet. I could go forever.

I try to convey my confusion to Jamie, and he just shrugs. I guess he doesn't know what's happening, either. Then the music comes up again, not a thumping electronic track this time, but a ballad. A slow song.

Jamie tilts his head. He doesn't know what to do, and neither do I. But I know what I want to do. Some folks vacate the dance floor, but others couple up, dancing hand in hand, arm in arm, fuzzy head on furry shoulder. I want that, and I want it with him.

So I ask him: “May I have this dance?”

He pauses, one paw on his chest, then nods softly. I try to conjure up my middle school dance lessons, placing my hands on his hips. He rests his forearms on my shoulders, a pleasant pressure I can feel through Archie’s fur.

Then I guide us as we sway, shuffling in a slow circle, staring into each other’s crafted eyes. It’s just as well that I can’t see his human eyes, can’t feel his skin on mine in this moment. I think I would explode if I did, or bolt and hide away. This is already almost too intense, my heart beating harder than it did when I was dancing at high speed.

And then Jamie pulls me closer. He holds my snout against his chest, his claws moving delicately down my back.

His embrace is so comfortable and warm, like the most luxurious pillow. I close my eyes, shutting out the rest of the world. It is only me and him.

And then it really is over. We reluctantly pull apart and file out of the building with the rest of the attendees. Only the smallest sliver of pink-tinged sunlight remains on the horizon.

Wordlessly, the two of us find a bench and sit together, our knees touching. We look together, not at each other, but at the sky.

"I'll be leaving the fursuit at home tomorrow," Jamie says. "Most years I only wear it for one day. I don't want to put too much strain on it."

"Oh, yeah. I'm a bit worried about the stress I've put Arcturus through today. I'm not sure how sturdy he really is."

"But I'll be seeing you tomorrow, won't I?"

"Of course!" I say. "The con's not over yet!"

"No," says Jamie. "Not yet."

We say our goodbyes and go our separate ways. I have no group for cover on my walk this time, but I'm so tired I don't care, and no one hassles me anyway. I strip in my hotel room and collapse into bed. Sounds like there's a party happening in another room, but I don't mind. The muffled music takes me back a few perfect hours, and I fall asleep smiling.

SUNDAY

Jamie's waiting for me when I arrive at the convention centre on Sunday. He's just himself: no claws, and a lot less fur. He seems to stand a little less tall than I remember from Friday. For my part, I'm a lot quieter, greeting him with a smile and then falling silent.

I just don't know what to say. How do I begin to talk about last night and what it meant to me? Should I acknowledge it at all? Or should I consider all that to have happened to two creatures named Jasper and Arcturus, not us?

We stick together, properly exploring the vendor hall this time. I pick up some souvenir buttons and some supplies I think I can use to improve Arcturus, all on sale as vendors try to liquidate before the end of the con. Jamie has a girl in the artists' alley do a sketch of Jasper, but it comes out too skinny, so I draw my own version of him with a fish in his mouth and we laugh it off.

We attend an anime screening, a board game hour, a history panel. We try mediocre cafeteria pasta, get snacks at a pop-up cafe attended by catgirl maids and catboy butlers. It's all fun, and we find our words, talking about the best fursuits and most interesting events. But every conversation trails off into reticence, all eye contact breaks in favour of staring at our shoes. There's so much I can't say.

And then it ends, and we find ourselves standing together again under a fading summer sky. Is this really it? Can I really let it end like this? I reach desperately for words and come up empty.

Jamie turns to me. "Are you hungry?" he asks.

"Yes," I say immediately, though I'm not at all.

"I know a place that's open late. It's a bit of a walk, though."

"I don't mind at all. It's a nice night," I say, though I would've gone along even if it were pouring rain.

He leads me away from the convention centre, getting us to a street lined with small businesses and fast food restaurants. Most of them look closed, though. His gait is long, but he slows down to keep pace with me, and we walk side by side. Our hands brush and I flinch.

"You sure this is okay?" he asks. "You have to check out in the morning, don't you?"

"Yeah, and early. But it's okay. I'm not tired yet," I lie.

"And then you're driving home, too. Or flying?"

I shake my head. "No, I drove. I'm in Grande Prairie."

"What's that, four hours away?"

"Closer to five, actually."

He's silent for a moment, then says, "That's not so far."

I smile. "No," I say. "It's not far at all."

We finally stop in at a donair place, empty but for two tailed teenagers seated at a small square table.

We greet them on our way to the counter, where Jamie orders a donair and I get a small poutine. He pays for mine before I can protest, so I drop a toonie into the tip jar.

We sit at a wobbly table in the quietest corner of the restaurant. The food's good, but I'm really not that hungry, so I pick at it one fry at a time.

"I've never been further north than St. Albert," Jamie says between bites. "Is Grande Prairie where you saw your Arctic fox?"

"Oh, no. They do dip into Alberta a bit but not that far south. I have family in Yellowknife, so I saw one up there."

"Oh, that's way north."

"I did say they like the North Pole! They're amazing at keeping warm. They can stand right on the ice without feeling pain. And then their coats thin out a lot during the summer so they don't overheat. They're really cute in summer, too, actually. Herrick was a jerk but I would love to make a summer Arcturus suit. It's probably not feasible to have one suit that changes, unfortunately, but how cool would that be?"

I break from my rant when I notice Jamie grinning.

"What?" I ask.

"Nothing."

"I went off the rails a bit, huh? I'll shut up..."

"No, don't. It's cute," he says, then takes a casual bite of his donair.

CUTE!

He thinks I'M cute.

My annoying rambling is cute.

Unable to look at him, I play with my poutine.

Jamie swallows his food. "Well, go on," he says.

"Sorry," I say with a nervous laugh, "all my fox facts seem to have up and vanished."

Despite my best efforts, I do eventually hit the bottom of my poutine. I drag my feet in tossing the styrofoam container in the trash and join Jamie outside.

"Let me walk you to your hotel," he says.

"Okay. It's right by the convention centre."

We begin the walk back, taking multiple streets silently. This is it. This is my deadline. If I don't say something in the next few blocks, I'll lose my chance. But still, still, my throat constricts.

No, I know I can do this, even without Archie's help. I can channel his courage. Even if I can't just come out and say it, I can start small.

"You know," I say, "when you first started talking to me, I thought you were probably just being nice to a new guy. And it seemed like you were friendly with everyone, so I told myself I couldn't take it personally. But... it meant a lot to me that you wanted to meet Arcturus. He's like a piece of my heart, you know? I don't really show people my art, and no one had ever seen my fursuit in person besides me. But you helped me be brave. I could do it because you were there. Because I wanted more than anything to open my heart to you."

He hasn't responded, and I've fallen a little bit behind. I can't see his face, but there, only a few metres down, my hotel looms.

I can't stop now.

I banish my embarrassment and take a deep breath.

"So I just... I just wanted to thank you. When my friend bailed I was dreading attending this alone, but you made it one of the most amazing weekends of my life."

My voice cracks at the end.

As Jamie slows to a stop, I close my eyes, squeeze my hands into fists, and command myself to get it together.

When I open my eyes, I see Jamie wiping tears from his.

"Oh shit, Jamie! I'm sorry, I didn't mean to—"

"It's okay. I'm okay," he says, sniffling and smiling. "I just really don't want this to be over."

So he felt it, too.

I pull him close to me and wrap my arms around him, placing my head on his chest. His fingers press firmly into my back.

He's so warm, and soft, even without an outer layer of fur. I could stay like this forever.

"I want your contact info," he whispers.

"Okay."

"And I've never been to Grande Prairie."

I smile into him. "It's not so far," I say.

"No," he says. "Not far at all."

www.ingramcontent.com/pod-product-compliance
Lightning Source LLC
LaVergne TN
LVHW090539110826
845146LV00003B/1181

9798233047848